P9-DYP-492

Oriole Park Branch
7454 W. Balmoral Ave.
Chicago, IL 60656
DISCARD

FIRST AMERICANS

The Cheyenne

SARAH De CAPUA

New York

ACKNOWLEDGMENTS

Series consultant: Raymond Bial

Marshall Cavendish Benchmark
99 White Plains Road
Tarrytown, New York 10591-9001
www.marshallcavendish.us

Map and illustrations by Christopher Santoro

Library of Congress Cataloging-in-Publication Data

Library of Congress Cataloging-in-Publication Data

De Capua, Sarah.
The Cheyenne / by Sarah De Capua.
p. cm. — (First Americans)
Includes bibliographical references and index.
ISBN-13: 978-0-7614-2248-8
ISBN-10: 0-7614-2248-X
1. Cheyenne Indians—History—Juvenile literature. 2. Cheyenne Indians—Social life and customs—Juvenile literature. I. Title.
II. Series: First Americans (Benchmark Books (Firm)
E99.C53D4 2006
978.004'97353—dc22
2006011967

Photo research by Joan Meisel
Cover photo: Dewitt Jones/Corbis
Art Resource, NY: 7, 15, 22, 23, 32, Werner Forman; Corbis: 1, 12, 28, 36, 39 Dewitt Jones; 16, 30, Werner Forman;
18, Canadian Museum of Civilization; 26, Gary Braasch; Getty Images: 33, 34; Raymond Bial: 4; The Granger Collection, NY: 11, 14.

Editor: Tara T. Koellhoffer
Editorial Director: Michelle Bisson
Art Director: Anahid Hamparian
Series Designer: Symon Chow

Printed in China
1 3 5 6 4 2

CONTENTS

LORY SC.

1 • WHO ARE THE CHEYENNE PEOPLE?

Many members of the Cheyenne nation live on one of two areas of land set aside for them by the U.S. government. One group, called the Northern Cheyenne, lives on a reservation in southeastern Montana. Another group, the Southern Cheyenne, shares land in Oklahoma with the Arapaho nation. Today, there are about 6,000 Northern Cheyenne and about 10,000 Southern Cheyenne.

The Cheyenne call themselves Tsitsistas (tsiss-TSISS-tahss), meaning "our people" or "people who are alike." The name "Cheyenne" may come from the Sioux word *Shai-ena*, which means "people of a different speech."

Hundreds of years ago, the Cheyenne lived in what is now Minnesota, near the **source** of the Mississippi River. They lived in villages along the river and grew corn, beans, and

After they moved to the Great Plains, the Cheyenne lived in tepee villages such as this one.

squash on farms. The woods provided them with materials for making shelters. The Cheyenne also hunted buffalo, deer, and other animals for meat, as well as for furs and skins to make clothing. Around the year 1700, tribes from the East moved onto Cheyenne lands. The tribes were mostly Ojibwe and Sioux, who had always been the Cheyenne's enemies. The Cheyenne were forced to move across the Mississippi River into present-day North Dakota. They built new villages and continued to live as farmers.

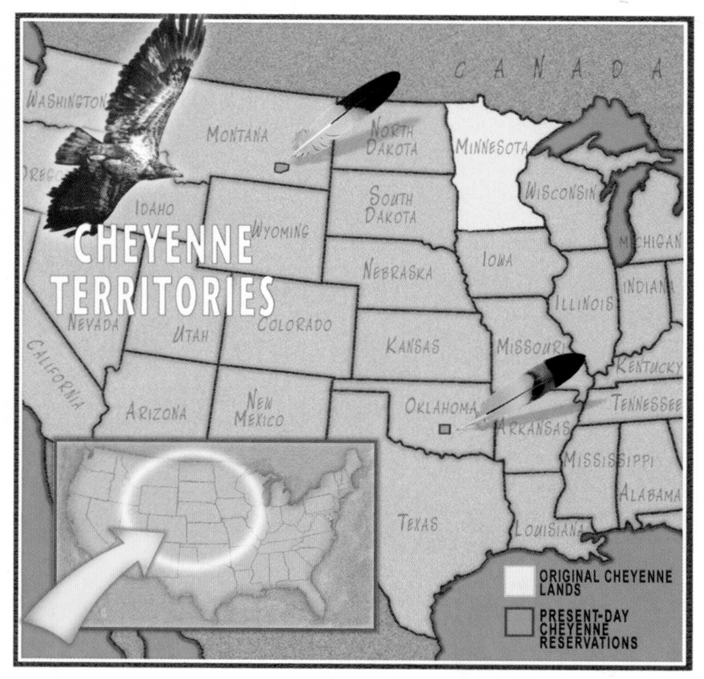

The Cheyenne lived first in what is now Minnesota and later moved to reservations in the present-day states of Montana and Oklahoma.

However, other tribes kept attacking the Cheyenne. After a while, the Cheyenne moved south to the Great Plains in what is now South Dakota. Once they moved, they began to live in tepees. These are cone-shaped structures made of wooden poles and covered with animal skins.

Around 1740, the Cheyenne began to capture horses from other tribes in the area. The horses were **descendants** of the horses Spanish explorers had brought to North America. The Cheyenne quickly became skilled horseback riders.

Another important change in the Cheyenne way of life came from moving onto the Great Plains. The plains contained millions of square miles of grasslands. A short, **hardy** grass called buffalo grass then covered much of the plains,

The Cheyenne were well known as good horseback riders.

which were home to herds of millions of buffalo. After finding the buffalo, the Cheyenne hunted them on horseback, and began to live as **nomads**.

The Cheyenne continued to move south and west, following the buffalo. Around 1832, the Cheyenne divided into two groups. The Northern Cheyenne stayed along the Platte River in present-day eastern Wyoming, northern Colorado, and western Nebraska. The Southern Cheyenne settled near the upper Arkansas River in what is now eastern Colorado and western Kansas.

Buffalo were very important to the Cheyenne way of life.

During the 1800s, the Cheyenne way of life changed again when large numbers of settlers moved westward. The settlers' way of life, which included building towns, roads, railroads, and fenced-in farms, interfered with the movements of the buffalo. The settlers did not understand how important the buffalo were to the survival of the Cheyenne. And the Cheyenne did not understand the white people's desire to settle the land.

Railroad tracks built through areas where buffalo roamed led to the death of many buffalo and changed the Cheyenne's way of life.

The settlers also brought diseases, such as cholera and smallpox. The Cheyenne and other Indians had no immunity to these diseases. That is, their bodies had no natural defenses to keep them from getting sick and, often, dying. In 1849, a cholera epidemic killed somewhere between 2,000 and 5,000 Cheyenne—about half of the members of one **band** of the tribe.

The U.S. government tried to help the Cheyenne and settlers live peacefully. The government made treaties with the

The Cheyenne and the settlers usually traded in peace, but their contact with each other exposed the Cheyenne to many diseases.

Cheyenne that were meant to protect their rights and keep them from fighting with the settlers. The treaties gave the Cheyenne food, clothing, tools, and other goods as payment for allowing settlers on their land. Sometimes, though, dishonest people from both sides broke the treaties. Cheyenne warriors attacked homesteads and killed families. White settlers took lands that the treaties said belonged to the Cheyenne and killed any Cheyenne they found living there.

The Cheyenne fought with the white settlers over land.

Beginning around 1857, the Cheyenne and the U.S. Army and local **militias** fought each other many times. Sometimes, Dog Soldiers—Cheyenne warriors known for their skill and bravery in battle—attacked first. Other times, the army or militias attacked first. The most famous conflicts occurred in 1864, 1868, and 1876. In 1864, the Colorado militia killed about 200 Cheyenne near Sand Creek in Colorado. This surprise attack came to be called the Sand Creek Massacre. In

The Battle of the Little Bighorn was fought on June 25, 1876. It was one of the few times the Indians defeated the U.S. Army in battle.

1868, U.S. Army troops attacked a Cheyenne camp along the Washita River in Oklahoma, killing about 100 Cheyenne. In 1876, Cheyenne warriors joined the Sioux in the attack on the U.S. Army at the Battle of the Little Bighorn, in present-day Montana. The warriors killed more than 200 soldiers commanded by George Armstrong Custer. Custer was also killed in the battle. Although the Little Bighorn was one of the few times that Indians won a battle against the U.S. Army, the Cheyenne knew they could not resist much longer. By the end of the 1800s, they gave up their way of life and moved onto U.S. government reservations.

George Armstrong Custer, who led the U.S. troops at the Battle of the Little Bighorn, was killed in the fighting.

The Buffalo Hunt

The Cheyenne and other Plains Indians had several ways to hunt buffalo. Before the arrival of guns and horses, they used spears and bows and arrows to kill one buffalo at a time. Using these methods, they killed many buffalo on every hunt. When the Indians needed to kill large numbers of buffalo, they used two methods: the buffalo pound and the buffalo jump.

Buffalo Pound: The buffalo were lured into a **ravine** by a hunter dressed in buffalo robes. Other hunters hid in bushes along the ravine, then stampeded the buffalo into a log corral so they could not escape. This made it easy to kill them.

Buffalo Jump: Hunters called "runners" or "chasers" herded buffalo toward a cliff, where other hunters waited behind rocks and trees. They waved blankets or shouted, frightening the animals and forcing them to run over the edge of the cliff. Hunters waited at the bottom to kill the injured animals.

The sites of several buffalo pounds are preserved at Buffalo Pound Provincial Park in southern Saskatchewan, Canada. The site of a buffalo jump is located at Badlands National Park in South Dakota.

The Cheyenne often used buffalo jumps to kill many buffalo quickly and easily.

2 · LIFE ON THE PLAINS

After the Cheyenne moved onto the Great Plains, they began to live in tepees. These shelters were better suited to their lifestyle of moving often to follow the buffalo herds. Tepees could be set up and taken down easily. Usually, three main poles made of pine formed the tepee's frame. Eight to ten smaller poles filled in the rest of the frame. Buffalo hides covered the tepee, and the doorway always faced east, toward the rising sun. Tepees were usually 18 to 20 feet (5.5 to 6 m) wide at the bottom. It took about 12 buffalo skins to cover a tepee. (The size of a tepee depended on how many people lived inside.)

The Cheyenne lived in small bands of family members. Each band had at least one chief. The chief was usually an older man, chosen for his wisdom, wealth, and courage. The chief kept order in the village and decided when the band

The Cheyenne began to build tepees after they moved onto the Great Plains.

would move. He also decided where the band would make its next camp and when to hunt buffalo.

Cheyenne families were made up of parents, children, grandparents, and unmarried aunts and uncles. Grandmothers helped with chores and looked after the children. Men were the heads of their families.

Most men in a band belonged to a warrior society. These societies included the Fox Soldiers, Chief Soldiers, Bowstring Soldiers, and Dog Soldiers. When a young man got married, he usually stayed with his father's band. This is because the Cheyenne believed that men who had grown up together worked well as a group because they had learned to have respect for one another.

The Cheyenne had many customs for all aspects of life, including life inside the tepee. When a band gathered for a meal, the men sat on buffalo rugs on the north side of the tepee. Women sat on the south side. The male head of the family sat in a special place at the back of the tepee. It was considered rude to walk between a person and the fire. Men ate their meals first. After they were done, the women and children ate.

The role of Cheyenne men was to hunt, make tools, and defend their families. Besides buffalo, the Cheyenne hunted antelope, deer, and elk. They trapped wolves and foxes for their fur.

Cheyenne women prepared animal hides to use as tepee covers, clothing, and blankets. Women put up the tepees and took them down. They gathered and prepared food for their families. Women and girls picked berries, seeds, and wild

Cheyenne women took care of their families, including preparing meals.

turnips. They also dried meat to make **pemmican**, a food that was important for survival for the Cheyenne. Women sewed clothing and moccasins for their families from animal hides. Sometimes, women went to war alongside the men. During a full-scale war, every member of the tribe—man, woman, and child—was present at a battle.

Cheyenne children were rarely punished if they misbehaved. Parents told their children what to do, and children

A Cheyenne woman scrapes a hide clean so it can be used as clothing, a tepee cover, or a blanket.

learned that good behavior earned the respect of others. Girls learned their role by watching and helping their mothers and other older women with their tasks. Boys learned by watching and imitating the actions of their fathers and the older men of the band.

Clothing was made from buffalo, deer, and elk hides. Women wore dresses, skirts, capes, and leggings. Men wore shirts, **breechcloths**, and leggings. After the arrival of Europeans, moccasins and clothing were decorated with glass beads obtained in trade. Children wore smaller versions of the adults' clothing. The Cheyenne also wore thick, heavy buffalo robes in cold weather.

A Cheyenne child wears traditional clothing.

Buffalo Burgers

This is a modern recipe for a traditional favorite Cheyenne food. Ask an adult to help you make it. Always wash your hands with soap and water before you begin.

You will need:

- 1 pound ground buffalo meat
- 1 tablespoon butter or vegetable oil
- salt and pepper, to taste
- 4 hamburger buns

Divide the ground meat into four patties, each at least 1/2 inch (1.3 cm) thick. Fry the patties in skillet with butter or vegetable oil for about 6 minutes on each side, or until it is no longer pink. Season the meat to taste with salt and pepper and serve on the buns, along with ketchup, mustard, lettuce, tomato, pickles, or anything else you would usually put on a hamburger.

Cooking Tip: Keep in mind that buffalo meat cooks faster, and at a lower temperature, than beef. So watch your burgers carefully to be sure they don't cook too long. Overcooked buffalo meat is very tough!

Black Kettle 1803–1868

Black Kettle was a Southern Cheyenne chief. In his youth, he was well known as a warrior. During the 1860s, he encouraged his people to seek peace with the settlers and soldiers. It was Black Kettle's camp that was attacked during the Sand Creek Massacre of 1864. Black Kettle escaped, and continued to work for peace. In 1867, he signed a treaty in which the Southern Cheyenne, Southern Arapaho, Comanche, and Kiowa received tribal lands in present-day Oklahoma. Both settlers and Indians broke the treaty, however. This led U.S. Army forces to invade Black Kettle's camp on the Washita River on November 27, 1868. Black Kettle and his wife were among the approximately one hundred Southern Cheyenne who were killed that day.

About one hundred Cheyenne were killed in the Sand Creek Massacre.

3 • CHEYENNE BELIEFS

The Cheyenne were very religious. Even today, many continue to follow some parts of their traditional beliefs. They believed in two main gods. Heammawihio, the Wise One Above, lived in the sky. He watched over the camp of the dead. Ahktunowihio, the Divine Spirit of the Earth, lived under the ground. He provided the Cheyenne with food, water, and plants.

The Cheyenne also believed that powerful spirits lived in all four directions—north, south, east, and west. Spirits lived in springs, streams, and on hills and bluffs. The Cheyenne believed in ghosts and underwater monsters.

Animals were important in Cheyenne beliefs. Eagles were symbols of spiritual strength and power. Bears were signs of good fortune. Mule deer and elk meant **endurance**. Many other animals were believed to be sacred, or holy. Most sacred of all

To the Cheyenne, buffalo were the most sacred of all animals.

was the buffalo, because it met so many of the Cheyenne's needs.

Two objects have long been at the center of Cheyenne beliefs. The Sacred Arrows are said to have been given to a Cheyenne named Sweet Medicine by Maheo, the Creator. The Southern Cheyenne are the keepers of the Sacred Arrows. The Sacred Buffalo Hat, also given to Sweet Medicine by Maheo, is kept by the Northern Cheyenne.

Major Cheyenne traditions include the Ceremony of the Buffalo and the Sun Dance. The Ceremony of the Buffalo was meant to ensure a good buffalo hunt. Warriors gathered in a **sweat lodge**. There, they smoked a sacred pipe and made food offerings to the spirits of the four directions. They sang, prayed, and feasted.

The Sun Dance was held in the late spring or early summer to renew the land. All the Cheyenne came together and built a special lodge for the ceremony. They sang, gave thanks to the spirits, and asked for protection from danger and illness. The Sun Dance lasted eight days. Modern Cheyenne still hold the

Sun Dance each summer.

The birth of a child was a happy event for the Cheyenne. Soon after birth, a child was given a baby name. When the child was five or six, his or her father planned a naming ceremony. If the child was a boy, the father's brother provided the new name. If the child was a girl, the father's sister gave her a new name. After the naming, the father of the child gave a horse to the person who had named the child.

As they grew up, girls played with dolls and toy

Cheyenne girls played with dolls such as this one.

Sometimes, a young man played a flute for the young woman he liked. If she liked his music and spoke to him, they became engaged.

tepees. They watched and helped their mothers and older women with their tasks. This taught them how to care for a family and home. As a girl got older, the women told her not to walk around the camp unless other adult women were with her. This was meant to ensure that others saw her as a proper young woman, so she could marry an upstanding young man.

As boys got older, they learned by watching their fathers and older men. Boys were given small bows and arrows, and learned to hunt by shooting small animals. At about age twelve, a boy's grandfather taught him about his duties as a man. Shortly after, the boy went on his first buffalo hunt. After a successful hunt, the boy could go to war.

If a young man liked a young woman, he waited for her when she went with the other women to get food or water. He tried to talk to her. If she did not stop to talk to him, he went away. If she liked him, she talked to him for several hours. If they decided to marry, the man took the bracelet the woman wore on her wrist. She allowed him to keep it as a sign that she was promised to him.

Cheyenne men and women did not exchange vows in a wedding ceremony. The woman was simply brought to the man's tepee and carried inside on a blanket. She was dressed in new clothes, and a large feast was held. The young couple's families exchanged gifts. One man might have two or more wives at the same time. The wives shared the chores, but each had her own tepee for herself and her children.

Although it was rare, divorce did occur among the Cheyenne. A couple could divorce if they didn't get along. To divorce, the wife just placed her husband's belongings outside the tepee.

When a person died, the family began a time of mourning

Beaded Prayer Fan

The Cheyenne used prayer fans for ceremonies and dances. The fans were made with colorful beads and eagle or hawk feathers. The Cheyenne were creative and artistic in the bead colors they used. You can make your own beaded prayer fan to help you show others what you've learned about the Cheyenne.

You will need:

- Several sheets of newspaper to work on
- A stick or piece of wood, about 12 inches long
- Thread or string, about 30 inches long
- Beads in any colors you choose (available at craft stores)
- Feathers (about 6–10) in any colors you choose (available at craft stores)
- Glue

1• Spread out newspaper to cover and protect your work area.

2• Glue the feathers around the tip of the stick.

3• Tie a knot at one end of the thread or string. String beads in whatever order or color pattern you choose until the string is completely beaded. Tie a knot at the other end of the string to keep the beads on.

4• Spread glue over the feather-tipped end of the stick or piece of wood, including the quills. Before the glue has a chance to dry, wrap the strand of beads around the stick, covering the quills.

5• Allow the fan to dry for several hours before you use it.

and prepared the body for a funeral. The dead person was dressed in his or her finest clothing, then wrapped in blankets or robes. People sang and prayed over the body. As a sign of grief, female relatives cut their hair. If a woman's husband died, she and the female relatives slashed their legs with hunting knives. Male relatives did not cut themselves, but they did unbraid their hair.

Sometimes, a warrior's personal belongings, such as bows and arrows or tomahawks, were placed by his body. Food offerings were also included, to comfort the soul. His finest horse was killed, so that its spirit could carry the warrior's soul to the afterlife.

A deceased person's body was placed in the branches of a tree or on a high platform made of branches and logs. In some cases, the body was hidden in a cave or buried under a pile of rocks. The soul would follow a path that led to the camp of the dead. There, the person's soul would join the souls of departed friends and family members.

How the Land and People Were Made

A long time ago, there was nothing in the universe except Maheo, the Creator, who has always been there. Once, the entire Earth was covered by water. There were fish and birds, but no animals. All the birds Maheo created were waterbirds, but they had no place to nest. Maheo realized this, so he commanded a great warrior to fall from the sky into the water, and told him to find the Earth's land. As the warrior floated on the surface, he called for all the waterbirds to dive under the water and search for the Earth. The swans, loons, and geese tried many times, but each failed. Then, a little duck dove under the water and, after a long time, surfaced with mud on its bill. The duck had found land. The warrior took the mud from the duck's bill and held it until it dried. Then he placed it in little piles on the water's surface. Each little pile grew larger and larger until it became land. The land grew into the great landmasses now called continents. Then, the warrior made a man and a woman. Later, he created other people to live on the Earth.

CHEYENNE INDIAN MUSEUM

4 • A CHANGING WORLD

Today, the Northern and Southern Cheyenne still practice many of their traditional ways. They maintain their language, religion, and unique identity as Native Americans. At the same time, they live in the modern world.

The Northern Cheyenne Reservation covers about 450,000 acres (182,000 hectares) of land. About one out of every five families lives in the rural areas of the reservation. The rest live in the small towns of Ashland, Busby, and Lame Deer, which are on or near the reservation. The reservation includes the site of an ancient buffalo jump, a burial ground of the great chiefs, and Custer's last camp before the Battle of the Little Bighorn. Dull Knife Memorial College, named after Chief Dull Knife, provides an opportunity for Northern Cheyenne to obtain higher education. There is also a museum

The Cheyenne Indian Museum is located at St. Labre Indian School in Ashland, Montana.

at the St. Labre Indian School in Ashland.

The Northern Cheyenne work as cattle ranchers, farmers, and producers of timber. They also keep a herd of a few hundred buffalo. Large amounts of coal were discovered on their land in the 1960s, but it has not been mined.

The Southern Cheyenne share land with the Arapaho. Their land covers about 85,000 acres (34,000 ha) near the

The Lucky Star Casino is owned by the Cheyenne-Arapaho Tribes of Oklahoma.

Washita Battlefield National Historic Site, near the Black Kettle National Grassland. Like the Northern Cheyenne, some Southern Cheyenne live in rural areas. Most live and work on farms in the towns of Concho, Canton, and Colony. They plant alfalfa and wheat crops. They also raise cattle, hogs, and buffalo. The Cheyenne-Arapaho Tribes of Oklahoma own and operate two casinos, in Clinton and

Modern-day Cheyenne continue to embrace their traditions.

Cheyenne Game

The Cheyenne have a traditional guessing game called the Hand or Stick Game. There are two teams. Each team has ten sticks. Each team also has a marked or colored stone. A team member places the stone in one hand without letting the members of the other team see who has it. The other team then has to guess which hand the player is holding it in. If the guessing team chooses the wrong hand, that team must give up one of its sticks. The object of the game is for one team to win all of the sticks.

Concho. These casinos provide much-needed jobs for the people, many of whom live in poverty. Natural gas and oil have been found on Cheyenne land. Drilling for these resources may help make life better for these tribes.

The Northern and Southern Cheyenne continue to find ways to make better education and jobs available for their people. Although many Cheyenne have become businesspeople, doctors, lawyers, and teachers, they still hold on to their traditions, especially those that have to do with the Sacred Arrows and Sacred Buffalo Hat. Proud of their past, the Cheyenne look to build a prosperous future.

TIME LINE

Before 1700 — The Cheyenne live as farmers in present-day Minnesota.

Early 1700s — The Cheyenne are driven from their lands by other tribes. They move first to present-day North Dakota, then to what is now South Dakota, and finally onto the Great Plains.

1740 — The Cheyenne capture horses and become excellent horsemen.

1800s — Large numbers of settlers begin to move onto Cheyenne lands.

1832 — The Cheyenne divide into two groups: the Northern Cheyenne and the Southern Cheyenne.

1864 — The Sand Creek Massacre takes place in Colorado.

1868 — The U.S. Army attacks the Cheyenne along the Washita River.

1876	1877	1884	1924	1960s	Early 2000s
Cheyenne warriors fight in the Battle of the Little Bighorn.	The Northern and Southern Cheyenne are moved to Indian lands in present-day Oklahoma.	The Northern Cheyenne Reservation is set up in Montana.	The U.S. Congress passes a law making all Native Americans U.S. citizens.	Coal is discovered on the Northern Cheyenne Reservation.	The Cheyenne-Arapaho Tribes of Oklahoma begin to operate casinos in Clinton and Concho, Oklahoma.

GLOSSARY

band: Group of family members.

breechcloths: Simple garments worn by men that reach from the waist to the upper thigh.

descendants: The offspring of people who lived long ago.

endurance: The ability to withstand a long physical, mental, or spiritual challenge.

hardy: Tough; able to survive under difficult conditions.

militias: Groups of people trained to fight, but who only serve in emergencies.

nomads: People who move from place to place.

pemmican: Dried meat (usually buffalo) that was pounded flat and was a favorite food of the Cheyenne and other Plains tribes. It could be stored for use during the winter months, so it was important for their survival.

ravine: A deep, narrow valley with steep sides.

source: The place where a stream or river starts.

sweat lodge: A dome-shaped hut in which sacred ceremonies are held.

FIND OUT MORE

Books

Bunting, Eve. *Cheyenne Again*. New York: Clarion Books, 2002.

Press, Petra. *The Cheyenne*. Mankato, MN: Compass Point Books, 2002.

Remington, Gwen. *The Cheyenne*. San Diego, CA: Lucent Books, 2001.

Santella, Andrew. *The Cheyenne*. Danbury, CT: Children's Press, 2002.

Web Sites

Cheyenne Indian

www.cheyenneindian.com

Northern Cheyenne Net

www.ncheyenne.net

Plains Indians

www.nps.gov/fola/indians.htm

INDEX

Page numbers in **boldface** are illustrations.

About the Author

Sarah De Capua is the author of many books, including biographies, geographies, and historical titles. She has always been fascinated by the earliest inhabitants of North America. In this series, she has also written *The Cherokee, The Iroquois,* and *The Comanche.* While researching this book, she enjoyed visiting the site of a buffalo jump in Badlands National Park, South Dakota.